ARRANGED MARRIAGE MAFIA

A Dark Italian Novel

MADISON KLIEN

Copyright © 2020 by Madison Klien

All rights reserved. No part of this book may be reproduced, stored in a retrieval system, or transmitted in any form or by any means, electronic, mechanical, photocopying, recording, scanning, or otherwise, without the prior written permission of the publisher.

Disclaimer

All the material contained in this book is provided for educational and informational purposes only. No responsibility can be taken for any results or outcomes resulting from the use of this material.

While every attempt has been made to provide information that is both accurate and effective, the author does not assume any responsibility for the accuracy or use/misuse of this information.

Table of Contents

ACT 1

   PILOT

   BUSINESS DEAL GONE WRONG

   CROSSING THE THRESHOLD

ACT 2

   A GUIDING HAND

   INDIVIDUAL DESIRES

   TEMPTATION

   DARK MOMENTS

ACT 3

   PERSONAL SACRIFICE

ACT 1

PILOT

Attention please, the last bus will be taking off soon . . . the female voice said through the public announcement system. Her voice was clear and audible.

She heard the announcement at the station and was in a hurry to on board the train. She picked up the pace in the direction of the bus. The other buses going her way had left except this one and it was getting late. The clouds were getting cleared as though it was giving a free invitation for the night to draw near. The next available bus would arrive in an hour but it could take much time. "No chance," she said. "It is not safe to be out alone in the city at night. No one wants to be the victim on the next evening news."

She could hear the engine of the bus rave as it was about to leave the bus stop. Carmela, a beautiful brunette with brown eyes and an appearance that looked out of place with the local dashed through to board the bus. She got the last ticket at the nick of time for a place called home. Home is usually a place filled with happy memories. But for Carmela, home was a place she would rather not associate with. However, it is the only place she knows as home at least until she is fully established on her own. Till she can stand tall. Although she is 5'5, she has a huge personality that makes her bigger in a room.

She clicks her heels on the pavement as she rushes to board the bus. *"What have we here?"* she thought. The bus was crowded with people packed like a tuna. Different kind of people with different shapes.

"All aboard," the driver says as she was the last person to get on the bus.

Carmela pushed her way through the crowd to find an available spot while holding her black-dyed hair from tangling with any unforeseen body. The bus began to move and so she stretches her hand to latch onto the bar above. The bus slightly lunges as it pulls away from the bus stop while she continued through the spaces between the people holding unto the bar to find a spot. Finally, she finds a spot after going through the many bodies with different foul odour and sweat from other people's body. The overpowering perfume that accompanies such smell made the stench thicker but she was not bothered.

She was focused on being her own person. It didn't matter if she had to lower the standards that she was born into. She was born with a silver spoon—she feels it was not deserving because of the source of her family's wealth. She doesn't approve of his ways. She has tried many times to persuade him from this life but he would not listen. He is the reason she set out to make her own merit, to make a path to follow and define her purpose. She knows it is a lot to do but she had set her mind on this endeavour.

She let her head down in the bus as they journeyed through the city while touching her softly shaped jaw as she thought about home. She would see him again. She thought, *"Will he listen to me this time or perhaps I could have some luck with him this time."*

She's been doing fine without him and enjoys the feeling of independence but she always thought he needed saving from his line of business. A business with so much bloodstain and what she would call blood money because of the illegitimate means by which it came by.

She admits to benefitting from the money while coming of age. The money funded her luxurious childhood and lifestyle. She knew nothing and had always thought it was normal. It is the reason for her fancy education and her social class in society. She always knew him as a businessman with security details protecting him from people who may want to hurt him. She later got to know better when she was enlightened. Since she knew about his dealings and how the money was made, she decided to cut herself away from all it.

The smell in the bus was unbearable but her mind was somewhere else. After a few stops, she pulls the rope and the bus slows down. The passengers had their eyes on the upscale community and they were marvelled. The look on their faces told they were all wondering: who could be stopping here?

People who lived in such a society do not take such a local bus. The door opens and a burst of fresh air was allowed into the bus and they could all smell the richness of the upscale society. The community is gated and well protected with security and surveillance systems.

The aesthetics and ambience were worth every gaze complemented with the magnificent structures insight. The clean pavement and the palm trees aligned were all symmetrical. It was clear that it was a specially designed community for the wealthy and upscale people in the society that are influential.

Carmela had to push her way through the crowd in the bus to reach the door. She got off the bus to the place she calls home. She heard whispers as the door of the bus was closing but she could not make out the words, though, she could tell it was all about her. She knew the feeling. It was not new and she was no stranger to such kind of reaction.

She looked at them with the back of her eyes as though she was not looking. It was written all over their faces. Questions about why she of such an upscale status would ride in a bus. The door of the bus closes and soon it departed. Carmela looks up and the view just had she saw it the last time she was there. The house is in a private and in a gated community with tall stone walls and precisely cut bushes. The home is vivid in color and style. She takes a deep breath and walks up to the gate. Carmela puts in her code followed by a clicking sound that shows that code was accepted. The gate opens up to her and she was flooded by a welcoming humid summer breeze that caressed her skin. This was one of her favourite things about her home. The cooling breeze that spreads around the house comes with a refreshing feeling.

She begins to walk to the house through the pathway with flowers on each side. It was about that time of the evening that the sun was setting. She looks up to admire the colours of the sunset spreading its hue across the sky. Its golden orange glow all over the horizon was beautiful to see.

She continues to walk with her brown eyes on the amazing sky view of the setting sun. She was happy and at that moment had cleared her mind of all the thoughts that was bugging her. Her moment and movement got hindered when she heard the sound.

"Good grief!" she sighed.

Something gave in on her left heel. She looks down in disappointment. She liked this shoe a lot but here it goes. Damned and destroyed. The heel of her shoe has broken and this was the last thing she would have thought would be a drag on her day. Her mood change in the instant as she was frustrated.

She continues as she walked unbalanced staggering until she arrived at the two-story home. She was faced with the huge door and she let herself in with her key. Everything seemed normal and nothing was out of place except the new portrait of him on the wall. Carmela closed the door and dropped her keys in a glass bowl next to the door.

She had her face down when she heard footsteps approaching in the hallway. She looked up slowly and watched him come her way. His presence filled the hallway with loud footsteps because of his size. He had a distinct lampshade moustache and thick eyebrows. He looked like a hired muscle with a nice slick back dark hair but his wealth conceals his overall appearance as he looked more of a big mafia boss. His arms are strong and from his body structure, you can tell that he had been through a lot of fights in his days. He was a man that did a lot of dirty jobs for the mafia. When you needed something done your go-to guy is Pasquale. He grew his reputation in the crime world and became a boss in his own right. He worked for all he had and was a success in this rig. This was all he had ever known. The life of organised crimes.

Everything he has done was for his only daughter Carmela who grew up to be a fine independent woman. He liked the woman she was becoming but he was different from her. He had a smile on his face and she could tell he was happy to see her.

"Hello, Father," she says. He embraced her in his warm arms. She is the only daughter that he has and all that he has got.

"Welcome home my daughter," Pasquale replies. I" thought you'd at least notify me that you were coming home. I would have had my boys bring you home."

"Not a problem, Father," Carmela responds. "I like to find my own way, you know I always do."

He laughed a little as he says, "That's my daughter. You are still as stubborn as always." Pasquale was dressed in a custom-tailored business suit complimented with a silk tie. It was as though he had just finished a meeting. She was happy to see him but she could not let out a smile. There was something on her mind. Her father saw it in her eyes. He had seen her this way before. He knew what she had in mind. Carmela already knew why he was dressed up that way. He had some illegal business dealings.

This was what she came for. To talk to him and there was no better time than right now.

"Father," she says, "when will this end? When will it all stop? When do I stop living in the shadows?" She began to voice her objection as she was upset.

Pasquale knew what she was on about from the moment he saw the look on her face. Carmela wants him to cut all his ties with the mafia.

"It's not time," he says. "It's not that easy," he added.

He listened to her, he heard her every word but it would seem to Carmela that her words are a broken record. It is a question she has often asked him but there was no changes nor response from him. She had given up on him ever-changing or leaving the mafia but she could never help it but ask him to leave whenever she sees him. She's afraid of what may happen to him especially with the law and the mafia.

Pasquale's words have always been the next verse to the song. He tells her it's not so easy and it became repetitive over the years. When he said this, it was nothing less than she had anticipated. Carmela still remained hopeful as she is a strong wield woman.

He kissed her on the forehead softly as he turns to leave but stops in the doorway when he notices one of his daughter's shoes has a broken heel. He was on his way out to another business meeting. The sound of the engine of the car brought forward to the doorway was his cue. But his attention was caught when he saw her broken heel. Then he turns to Carmela and tells her, "You could use another shoe. Let me call the manager at the store to deliver you their finest shoes immediately." He brings out his mobile phone to scroll through his contacts. But Carmela touched his hand to get his attention. She appreciates the offer but tells him she prefers that he doesn't buy her any more shoes. Pasquale understood what her gesture was all about. She wanted to find her own path and create her own merit. To buy what she wanted on her own. He respected her decision but did not say a word about this.

His expression went blank as he turns and leaves. "I will see you later," he says. He opens the door and his security details were set and ready. The opened the door to his black SUV to let him in. And soon they set out for his next meeting.

Carmela goes up to her room to change into something more comfortable. She has a huge mirror wall in her closet where she admires the woman she had become. Speaking confidently to herself in a monologue, she says, "I can do this, I got this."

She is a 26 years damsel with a unique birthmark at her left lower eyelid that makes her appearance more compelling and beautiful. Her fair skin makes her more attractive with her dominant personality. She looks in the mirror to clean her face with face wipes. Her square face makes her look bold with her softly shaped jaw. She cleans her face nicely with the wipes all around her well-formed nose and full lips. After she was done cleaning her make up with the natural-looking foundation off, she went further to change from her ambiguous clothes to evening wear. The evening wear was earth coloured which was long and flowing to compliment her long legs.

She had a long day and journey and so she was very hungry. She packed her mid lengthy curly braided hair with a rubber band and proceeded down to the kitchen. He goes into the fridge to pick out salad and chicken to microwave.

As the chicken heat up in the microwave, she waited to sort out a portion of salad in a bowl. Then soon after, the timer beeped as the roast chicken was ready for serving. Carmela took her dinner to the living room and she turns on the TV. She switches from one channel to the other with the remote control until she stumbled on a Breaking news of an ongoing homicide being reported live. There were yellow tapes indicating it was a crime scene with several reporters and law enforcement agency in the background. Two bodies were found dead in the middle of a park. The report says they were shot in the head as though it was an execution but nothing was confirmed. Other observers testified that they heard two sounds of gun shot that followed at intervals. They had no leads and no suspects. These kinds of reports have been aired many times. There was a time her father was covered in blood when he got home and there was a news about a shootout and dead bodies. The news was similar to the one aired tonight. Carmela could not help but worry that her father could be involved in the shooting aired on TV. Her father left the house as though he was going for a meeting but Carmel had a hunch that he was up to no good. She hopes he doesn't get himself into any form of trouble. He is the only family that she has and she couldn't afford to lose him.

As the news continued on, Carmela could not help but think that the hit was carried out by the mafia, and more so, that it was done by her father.

BUSINESS DEAL GONE WRONG

After her meal, she felt heavy and tired. She had a long day and the stress was weighing on her. Most especially the stress from the travelling on the bus. The TV news was all about tragic events, death and more violence all over the world. The world did not feel safe and yet she lived in a home where her father contributes to the dangers in it. No matter how she tried to dissociate herself, she would always be in this world. She grew up in it and the only way she can truly be free from all of it is if her father would quit or retire from the mafia. He has been loyal to them for years. He should be able to get hall pass or they could travel to somewhere far away to start anew. Her eyes were getting heavy and so she went up to the bathroom for a shower before going into her room to get the rest she deserved. She cleaned up nicely and got into her nightwear after which she goes to tuck herself into bed while covering all of her body except her head under the duvet. She was busy reading some emails on her phone when she slept off without doing what she'd set out to do—sleeping into the night. It was peaceful with dreams of the future she had pictured and she was happy but not for long. She hears a loud bang as though a door was slammed. She wakes up to the loud sound coming from down the stairs.

"What is it this time?" she thought as she was terrified by the sound. She heard heavy studs of a sound climbing up the stairs. The sound got louder and louder till there was another slam and the sound began to fade away into silence. It was late into the night. She did not think to check the time but it was clear that it was late. Her instinct was to investigate what was happening. *"Call the police. Nah not an option,"* she thought. It was never going to be an option to call the law enforcement to their home. Especially with the kind of man her father was, the police is the last resort. She can handle this, she was sure.

Carmela jumped out of bed quickly like a springing cat. She reached out for her baseball bat that was close to the bedroom door. She was given the bat by her father as a gift. As a kid, she loved to watch baseball and she was a huge fan of the Yankees. She would go out supervised to play the game with the boys. She was an excellent pitcher and also a good first base player. But that was all in her past, as she grew up, she played less of the game. Carmela had a good grip of the bat and she has a good swing when it comes to it. She was not rusty, she still had a good swing in her. She had no trouble with the curve when she played and so she will have trouble smashing the head of any intruder. She is brave and courageous yet when faced with danger, she was frightened. Yet, over the years, she has learnt to face her challenges head-on. The sound from the staircase had reduced. Carmela rushed out of her bedroom into the passageway but there was no one? She was barefooted and so it made her steps easy and soft on the ground. She made no noise with her movement. The lights were on and she began to move slowly towards the stairs. There was a trail of blood leading all the way to the bathroom. She held onto the bat tightly ready to swing if the need arises as it seemed there was an intruder in the house. Her once heavy sleepy eyes were cleared and she was very much awake and alert at the looming threat. The light in the bathroom was on. Carmela could recall turning it off before going to sleep.

Suddenly she heard the sound of running water in the bathroom. It sounded like it was coming from the shower. She slowly pushes the door open and then completely opens the bathroom door wide. The sound got louder as the shower was turned on to the max.

She noticed clothes on the bathroom counter, she could not recognise the clothes. It was different from the clothes her father wore on his way out. She remembered clearly that he was wearing a bespoke suit. Many thoughts ran through her mind.

She hoped he was okay and not badly hurt or in any danger. The blood trail was leading into the shower and she could hear slight grunts coming from behind the shower curtain.

It would seem there was no danger that required the solution of the baseball bat. Carmela placed the bat against the base of the wall as she moved silently into the bathroom with slow walking. She made no sound as she approached the shower.

She was truly worried and terrified. But his silhouette showed he was standing so she thought he must be okay. He had to be, she reassured herself as though it would change anything.

"Dad!" she whispers but no response.

"Dad!" she calls out his name again, yet no response and she became more worried. She moved closer and there was silence but only the sound of the running shower and her heartbeat. She stretched her hand towards the shower curtain. She held onto it and took a deep breath as she slowly began to pull the curtain back.

There he was - her father.

Pasquale was clothed in his full attire. He looked as though he was soaked in a pool of blood. She watched the shower pour on him to wash away the blood on his body and she watched the water push the blood into the drain. He was okay and in good health. Carmela was relieved but her concern grew more.

Whose blood was it? What had he done this time around?

Her father once told her the less you know the better. So no questions asked about what had happened. She knew the drills. He would take care of it. He always does. This is the reason he had been in the game for so long. It was just another rough night. She had seen worse and this was nothing much compared to what she had seen. However, she never knew the story behind what has been happening.

Her father realising that she had come around continues to look forward as though she was not there. He did not acknowledge his concerned daughter next to him. Carmela understood, it has always been this way. They don't talk about his business or what happens. But it would seem something was not right. *"What could have gone wrong?"* she thought as she proceeded to assist him.

She placed her hand on his cheeks as she gently turns his gaze to focus on her. She needed him to confide in her. Although she wanted him out of the crime business, she still wanted him to trust her. She began to speak softly to assure him where she stands. She is with him and would be there for him no matter what. He is her father and there is no one that can ever replace him in her life. He didn't say a word but continued to gaze at her in bewilderment. Carmela picks up a clean towel in the bathroom to clean up the residue blood on his face and other parts of his exposed skin that had bloodstains. She had never seen him this way. Pasquale was stunned. It was the first time he would be this way and it made her think of what could have happened out there. She helps her father out of the tub as he put his hands around her. She led him to his room and helped him to pick out clothes to wear. She gave it to him then made her way out of the room to wait for him. Pasquale changed into the clothes while Carmela was outside waiting for him, a little shaken and relieved at the same time. She had a weird and strange feeling about the night.

Moments later, he opens the door and it was as though he was himself once again. Carmela did not have to be told. She knew what to do. She went into the room to take his soaking wet clothes and the towel she used to mob his skin. She took the clothes to the fireplace where she would set it on fire. She lights up the fireplace and soon the fire was up. She throws the clothes into the fireplace and she watched the fabric burn in the rising red hot flames. As the clothes burns, she notices she had some blood on her night top and so she takes it off and throws it into the fire. This was a crime that needed some covering up. She knew about crime and so she got a mop stick and bucket with disinfectants to clean the bloodstains from the door up to the stairs and to the bathroom and the bathroom floors. She also cleaned the door handles and railing of the staircase. Every evidence had to be destroyed. These were the things she learned from her father from his endeavours. This she knows about crime; it comes back to bite you in the ass if the evidence is not properly disposed of.

She was sweaty from the cleaning she had done and so she took a quick shower then returned to her room. She changed into another nightwear after which she decides to return to check on her father. She got to his door and knocked but there was no response. Then she leaned into the door and she began to hear him talk. It was not audible but she could tell he was on a phone call talking to someone. She could not tell exactly how intense the conversation was but it sounded very serious.

Moments later, she heard the door unlocking. "That took longer than expected," she said.

Her father comes out with a straight face as always with his phone still in his hand. In the morning or at the dead of the night, his face was always straight. He rarely smiles which gave him a stone cold facial look. He walked up to her to say some words. Carmela had seen this face before. He was about to tell her something serious or give her and instruction with no questions asked. She wondered why everything about her father was never straight forward. It always comes with poking questions which can be tiring as she would never get an answer if she asked. And if she did get an answer it will not make any difference and so she had learnt over the years to not ask any questions. However, she would always voice her opinion when she had the opportunity. They have been on this journey for such a long time. She knows her father and she understands him. He cleared his throat and he began to speak.

"I just had a long phone conversation and this is what you need to know," he says.

Oh, dear! She sighs without words but her face says it all.

"Don Vito is on his way here."

Carmela's eyes were in disbelief. "The Don Vito!" she exclaimed. Her father never wants her around when the Don comes to the house. She knew already that she would have to leave the house that night. Tonight could not get any better. Good grief! She sighed . . .

"The mafia boss is on his way to our home."

"Yes, indeed," he said.

Don Vito Agresti is the most feared mafia boss in the city. She had read about him in the papers and on the news. The authorities had nothing on him. He had the city in his pocket and he ran a successful criminal enterprise and organised crime. If he is personally coming to your home it means you should fear for the worst. He doesn't go visiting except when he had a business he wanted to see through to the end. But what business could he have with Pasquale that he needed to see its completion at this time of the night. It had to be serious for Pasquale to be so shaken up that he wanted his only daughter away from the scene because of the worst case scenario that could happen. He needed to get her away from everything that was about to go down tonight. What could her father have done? What mess had he gotten himself into? There was no time to think. What were they supposed to do now?

He told her she had to leave the house immediately. He gave her a key to a safe house and asked her to take one of the cars in the house. Carmela knew the safe house, she had been there before when she was younger. She could recall they went there for a night. Now that she thinks about it, she could only think that they were there hiding from someone or to lay low till things got back on the upside.

She knew the car he wanted her to take. It was the one that was registered in her name and it looked like a commoner's vehicle which would not look out of place in any neighbourhood as it was an affordable car. The car is a stick just the way she liked it. It was late into the night and all of these were happening. This was her world. This is her home. It is different from the memory other kids had growing up in their homes. Home came with a lot of responsibilities for her. It could also be a battle field and no error could be made at home. This is home where anything could happen. The unpredictable happens in what she calls home. She loved to stay away but this would forever be home. It was barely a day since she got home and she could not get a good night sleep before the troubles came running back into her life.

She heard his instructions clearly and she affirms to it. Carmela nods her head and says, "Yes, Father," without questioning him. She set out to her room to get her things to leave immediately at his request. On her way to pack her things, she had other ideas. *"I have to convince him to come with me,"* she thought.

CROSSING THE THRESHOLD

He followed her immediately as she left his presence. Carmela was halfway to her room when he made his move. And in a haste, he dashed to her room behind her. Carmela hurriedly picked a suitcase which she drew closer to her closet. She began to throw random clothes from her closet into the box. She was surprised to see her father join her.

"Hurry," he says. "Take some essentials."

Carmela looked at him as he assisted her. She holds his hand to get his attention. He looked at her and then she says, "Come with me Father. Let's go together. Let's leave all of this behind. Let's go somewhere to start anew."

"Come with me. . ." she pleaded with him. She begged as her eyes were teary but she held back the tears. Her father never brought her up to cry. It's a sign of weakness and she is strong. She had to be stronger than ever.

She had what she needed and her father began to line the zipper of the bag.

He turned to her with his hands running through her hair. He says, "Carmela, my child. All I do is to protect you and give you the life that you deserve, but not like this. I can't protect you if I should go with you. So I will stay. This is the only way I can protect you. I can't do what you ask of me."

Her eyes burned from the tears flowing from her eyes. She was taught to be stronger but she gave in to the emotions as she could no longer hold it in. the tears flowed down her face but her father did not react to her tears. Pasquale picks up the bag which was now full and shoves it into her arms. "Follow me," he says, "and hurry up," as he led her to the living room. "You know what to do right."

"Yes," she says.

"Now run the drill with me," he instructed.

Carmela began to narrate how she would get to the safe house. "I will drive the car to the bus stop then park at the corner. I will leave the vehicle then board the bus leaving for the suburbs."

"Very good," he says. "You will be fine my child. You are brave. I need you to leave without looking back. Can you do that Carmela?"

"Yes, I can Father," she says as she nodded her head in acknowledgement. She tried again to persuade him. "Father! Come with me. Please change your mind and come with."

He followed her up to the door while holding her. He held her face with his two hands to plant a kiss on her forehead. He only needed to bend a little has her head was on his chest level. "Stay safe," he says. He watched her step outside completely as he pushed her then he slams the door on her. She heard a sound that followed and she could tell that the door had been locked from inside. She thought to knock the door. She wanted to be in but what was she thinking. She knew he would still not open the door for her nor hear whatever she had in mind. Her thoughts were finding her way to the car and drive away until her taillights were no longer visible to anyone because of the mile she would have covered. She would have one hand on the wheel and the other on the gear for changing the transition at each increase or decrease in velocity.

She would keep the bag on the passenger seat with thoughts that her father could be driving and she would be riding shotgun with him. That was just wishful thinking.

Carmela turns around to find herself staring at the barrel of a gun pointed between her eyes. Her heart began to race, her breath was seized at the moment then it began to drag. There were several young men around. She was too terrified to count them but they wore a black 3-piece suits and flat caps.

The man in front of her made a hand gesture that she should remain calm. Pasquale notices the sudden silence outside and he knew immediately that some men were around. He unlocked the door and steps outside. More men point their gun at him to put him under control. He knew there was no chance for him to take them on his own. His fear was his daughter could be caught in the middle of a gunfight if it were to happen. She was taken to the car to drive. The man with the gun pointed at her with instructions to drive and not call any attention to them. If she did, Pasquale would be killed first before they execute her. Carmela looks at the front door where she sees a huge man lead her father into the car. He looked like a hired muscle. She watched as he was taken to the car where he sat on the passenger's seat. The man was also well dressed in a suit with a flat cap. Carmela sat on the driver's seat while two men sat at the back.

"Drive!" one of the men says authoritatively, as though he had other places to be at this hour.

"Again," he says, "if you try to signal for help, both of them will be killed instantly."

Carmela follows the men's instructions fully, making sure she doesn't act out or draw attention, for the fear of death casts out any doubt. They told her where to follow and every turn she had to cut into. Some of the roads were new to her but she continued to drive as instructed by them. She thought to ask where they were going but it would pointless. So she continued to drive all the way. She would make attempts to look at them through the mirrors but they cautioned her to focus on the road. Sweaty palms and scared to her marrow, Carmela could only think of the worst. They instructed on where to turn and what part to follow to avoid street cameras. She drove slowly and so the journey seemed very long.

Suddenly she was told to park by the roadside in the middle of nowhere she could identify as it was dark.

"Get down!" they instructed and she did. Then she heard a beep sound. There was another car by the road. A black saloon vehicle. Carmela and her father were brought out of the car both helpless, unable to do anything. The men went on to cover their eyes with a piece of black fabric. Then they shoved them into the other car at the back seat. They knew not where they were going all through the journey of the night. But Carmela was able to get a glimpse through the loosely woven dark fabric. She could see light trails of a streetlight. She could tell they were no longer on the empty road but in an actual city, town or neighbourhood perhaps. Between being scared and terrified of the unknown, Carmela could not tell how long they had been on the road. Suddenly, the car began to slow down till it came to a stop.

There was silence but only the slight vibration and sound of the car engine as it was still running. The next sound was a squeaking sound and it was like that of metal clanks and she could tell that a gate was opening up. The car was put back into gear with a little jerk moment and soon it began to move slowly into the compound till it came to a stop. The engine was turned off and the doors in the car were opened. Carmela and her father were both dragged out of the car. The men went ahead to remove their blindfolds and for a moment they squint their eyes as there was a bright light coming from the giant building up ahead. They began to see clearly as their pupils adjusted to the suddenly bright light rushing into their eyes. It was a large two-story home and the remaining surrounding was in pitch darkness except for the spot they were. There were security cameras that could be seen at each angle. The house seemed to be heavily fortified with state of the art security and equipment. The men pushed them forward to indicate they start moving and they were both escorted into the building. The entry way was spacious with marble finishing and high ceilings with decorative embellishment and there were huge paintings on each sides of the wall with golden ornamental frame. There were artefacts and scented flowers that could easily be seen in the large and spacious hall. They took them down the hallway and into a corner before stopping at a black door. They were taken into this room which had dimmed lights and no windows. The room smelled of death, hell and something more unspeakable. The walls and floors were made of metal. The room seemed like a torture chamber where the mafia used to extract the truth or kill anyone that crossed them. Carmela could not tell what the room was used for but her instincts told her it was bad. It was really bad. They were screwed. She was scared and her heart as though it was almost ripping itself out of her body as it continued to beat faster.

Carmela began to think of the many different ways it would end terribly. She thought of the ways it would end that would not hurt much but no matter how much she thought about it, it was going to hurt very much.

"Oh god!" she sighed silently. "Oh! God," she cried silently. All she thought about was her end. The men tied her to a chair and also her father. They tied them so tightly they could not move any part of their body. They were completely restrained like animals. They were gagged as well as unable to speak but could only mumble words. They were placed across the room to face each other. The men then left them alone as they stepped out. They could only think of the worst that would happen next when the men would return to the room. Pasquale looked into the eyes of his daughter who was terrified. His face was emotionless but he felt some pain as he had failed to protect her from this life. He felt he had failed her and it broke him much more. Carmela's expression was full of worry and fear. It would seem they will die together. She was sure of this,

They were sure of this. They got sweaty and their clothes was gradually getting soaked in those sweat areas. Moments later, three walked into the room one after the other. The first man terrified Carmela as she could remember he pointed a gun at her earlier at the house. Then another man followed who was carrying a baseball bat and a black suitcase.

Finally, the third man comes in and Pasquale sat up as best as he could. The man introduced himself as Don Vito. Pasquale knew that but Carmela had never met him before. She knew him only by the name. His presence was intimidating. He looked around the room and as he did, he spread some fear. Then he collected the bat from his muscle and observed it as though it was something he had never seen before. He liked the smooth surface. He rubs it with his palm then grips the bat by the base and swings it in the direction of Pasquale to hit the head.

"No!" Carmela cried through the gag.

Pasquale was in pain as he bled. He yelled so loudly. Carmela had never seen her father in so much pain in all her life. It hurt her to see him getting hurt. He bled on the side of his head as he had his face down with so much discomfort as he could not hold where it hurt. The blood flowing from his head was now staining his clothes.

"Silence!" Don Vito yells to stop Carmela from crying. And she does immediately but with tears still flowing from her eyes.

The Don began to speak. He likes to make an entrance with fear and intimidation. He liked to hurt those who got in his way. Loyalty is just a currency. He burns it the moment a line has been crossed with no exceptions.

"Did you think you would get away with it?" Don Vito

says with his voice having a subtle anger tone. "Did you think that? You thought wrong." He pushes Pasquale up so that he could look into his eyes as he talks.

"Answer me!" he shouts.

"Boy oh boy ... who could have thought that you would betray me? Death means nothing to me," Don Vito says. "You killed the most important client for the Mafia. You have set us back by a decade for your action. I am going to enjoy this," he says. He picks up the bat once again and this time he hit Pasquale's stomach and he screamed as loud as he could through the gag. The gag began to soak up with blood flowing from his head.

Carmela screams through her gag as she could no longer stay silent. She begged for his life with the gag in her mouth and gestures on her face.

Pasquale was trying to cough out blood which soaked the gag much more. He was sweating and in dismay.

The man with the black briefcase laid it down on a metal table and releases the locks and opens it. Carmela became more terrified when she saw the horrific tools in the box. She saw sharp metal and other tools she had never seen before.

Don Vito walks over to the briefcase to pull out a knife shining in the dimmed room. Then he walked back to Pasquale. He taunted him with the knife before walking over behind him. He used the knife to cut his leg slowly and more blood spilt out from Pasquale who screamed out through the gag in his mouth.

Uncontrollable tears flowed through her eyes and her vision became blurred. She felt helpless and wish there was more she could do beside beg for his life. Her father was losing blood and she feared so much for his life.

The muscle who carried the black briefcase turns to her to hush her from making more noise. He goes into the briefcase to pick up a sharp object that looked like a corkscrew. He held it firmly in his hand as he approached her. He pointed the sharp object at her and maid partial contact as he tells her to be quiet. Then he began to apply pressure on her body as he dug into her skin. She cried from the pain and more tears flowed from her eyes.

The other man who pointed the gun saw this happen switched his thoughts and without much thinking, he gets involved and pushes the man away from hurting her. Don Vito paused to observe as he noticed what was happening. He pulls the younger man to his side and whispered something to him.

Carmela had no idea of what was happening or what they said but by their body movement, she could deduce they were talking about her. It would seem they have decided to kill her off immediately because of her behaviour. *"This is the end,"* she thought.

Don Vito began to walk toward her with his intimating look and appearance. Carmela could smell the sweat from his forehead along with the smell of her father's blood that had paltered on his cloth.

Then he says to her, "Today is your lucky day," as their eyes met. "She is to be spared," he orders the big guy. "However, your freedom to live, to see the sun again and exist comes with a price. You will be marrying my son - Salvatore. You have a strong resolve and you will make an excellent wife for him. It would be an honour for you as you shall accept this offer to live."

He calls his name, Salvatore, and he answers, "Yes, Father." Carmela was surprised that he was the one who pushed the big guy away and also the man that pointed the gun to her at her home. Don Vito instruct Salvatore to untie her immediately. He unties her and pulls her up from the chair with her mouth still gagged. Carmela was more concerned about her father as her eyes were on him and she mumbled some words through the gag. Salvatore understood what she was trying to tell him and immediately he tells her it is no longer her concern.

"Now, come with me," he says as he leads Carmela to her room.

Pasquale was in continuous torture and Carmela could hear his muffled screams through the gag and the metal chair jerking vigorously. As she was being taken away from the room, she turned to look him before the door was shut behind her. She was scared for his life.

ACT 2

A GUIDING HAND

She kept hearing his cry as she was taken away. The farther they moved, the fainter the sound of his pains and cries. Salvatore instructed her not to worry about it as worrying won't make any difference. "He got what's coming to him," he said. "I must say, he is lucky Don Vito hasn't executed him yet. So stay with me. My father has been generous to spare you."

Her eyes were heavy yet all she could think about is her father. *"Lucky!"* She thought about what that even means. She kept her inner voice to herself. They continued together through the hallway that leads to a staircase. She thought to make a run for it but that would mean the end of any hope her father will have to be alive. The path was scented with oil perfume and it had ancient artworks that would cost a fortune in the market. He led her up to the stairs and she could see more cameras at each angle she turned her head. Finally, he takes her to a room.

"This is your room," Salvatore says to her. She walked slow and sluggish but he encouraged her to brace up. The room was huge with artworks and a huge mirror. She could tell the room was designed for a woman. The floor was easy on the feet as she walked into the room. Although beautiful in sight, her mind could not get over the torture her father was undergoing. The room had a king-sized bed with beautiful ornaments on the frame. She strode to the bed and crawled into it till she got to the edge of the bed. She scanned the room with her eyes to find any camera but none was visible. It would seem there were no cameras in the room. She took a deep breath then another, trying in a view to calm her nerves. It wasn't working. She was shaking up and panicking.

The picture of her father bleeding was in her head. She picked up a white fluffy pillow and she put it on her lap with her legs crossed as she sat on the bed. She held it tightly with both hands as she squeezed her frustration into it. She became angry about being helpless and unable to do anything to save him. She could not make a decision for herself except the option given to her by Don Vito. No goes against the Don. He says what he wants and he gets it. This wasn't how she planned her life. She wanted a life away from the mafia. Now the mafia is bringing her into the life she wanted out of. Don Vito has set her up for his son. Like everyone one captured against their will all she began to think about was her escape. The more she thought about it the more she thought about her father. It broke her heart much more. Her situation is hopeless. She was at the bottom of despair and so she looked up to the ceiling with her heavy eyes and tears began to race down her cheeks. As it seemed her father had a 50/50 chance at life or death. She was by herself when she heard footsteps and it would seem it was more than a person coming to her.

"What could be happening now? Is he okay?" she hoped. The door began to open slowly and her heart started to race. Hope is truly a dangerous thing for a woman like her. The intimidating personality appeared before her. It was Don Vito but this time he was accompanied by someone else. A woman whom he introduced to her as his wife. She looked colourful in

her dress with her beautiful olive skin. Carmela wiped her tears as she stood up from the bed as though everything was alright. She had to be fearless. Carmela expressed her concern as she demands to know what had happened to her father.

"Tell me what you've done with him," she said. "Where is he?" she demanded. Although she was scared of him, she did not let that hold her back from demanding an answer from him.

Don Vito did not like her tone. Carmela could sense she was getting on his nerve. She felt good about it for a moment. Her sharp tone irritated the mafia boss. But she had no idea what it means to disrespect a mafia. Don Vito descended on her face a slap that left a mark on her cheeks which saw her face turn in the instant. She touched her wounded reddened cheek with her right hand and her eyes opened. With a wave of foolish anger and bravery, she said again with a sharper tone, "Tell me about the fate of my father now!"

The Don looked at her with so much disgust in his narrow dark blue eyes as he hit her again, much harder, with a slap that sent her flying onto the bed.

She became scared as she was lying flat on the bed and crawling backwards on the sheets as Don Vito began to walk closer to her with his intimidating presence. His eyes lit like it was on fire from hell especially with his tapered eyebrow.

"Child!" he said with a heavy voice. "I will spare you today because you are not familiar with how things are done here. I understand you have not had the opportunity to learn your place in the mafia. I will give you a pass tonight. This is your chance to get acquainted with the mafia. The first rule and the most important rule is never to disrespect me. The next rule is never to disrespect your future husband. Do you understand?" he yelled at her.

"Yes, sir," she cried.

Don Vito continued to walk towards her with brewing anger and Carmela started to draw backwards. A soft hand touched Don Vito by the shoulder. He looks over to his beautiful wife – Maria. She stepped in to calm his nerve. She is the only one capable of doing this. She had this effect on him. "My love," she says, "do not let out your anger on her as she is but a child that knows nothing. Would you leave her to me?" she suggests.

He looked at her and saw to reason with her. Cold with no emotion as though he was not moved by her words, he said, "Very well then, I will leave you to this. Keep her in line," he commanded her. He held her by the face and planted a soft kiss on her forehead. She reassures him that she will take her in and explain to her to understand the new life she has been brought into. He looked at Maria once more and nods his head. Then he leaves the room by slamming the door on them. That was not enough, he continued by locking the door behind him.

After the door was locked, Maria ran up to her to ask if she was okay. "How are you feeling my child?" Carmela was dumbfounded without saying a word as many thoughts went through her mind. Maria looked out of place as the wife of the mafia boss because she had a warm and caring feeling. Maria touched her face checking if she was okay. Carmela's visions were blurred from the slap and her hearing were distorted that she could barely make out the words of Maria. Her eyes started to open as she saw the frame before her with a rounded jaw and a square face. Maria looked more beautiful up close as Carmela's eyes began to normalise. She saw into her slanted brown eyes which showed so much concern. "Are you alright?" Maria asked again.

Arrrg! Ouch! Carmela sighed as she touched her cheeks. The reality of her situation became more obvious that she could no longer elude it with a brave attitude. She was in no place to demand anything. Carmela got up to sit at the edge of the bed as Maria was trying to nurse her hurt cheek.

Suddenly, Carmela fell on her knees and began to cry. She kept sobbing that Maria had to tell her that crying won't get her any help. Maria was not sure if anyone was listening as from her experience in the mafia especially at Don Vito's house, anyone could be watching and listen and so she leaned closer to Carmela like she was helping her only to whisper in her ears, "Women stick together." After she said this, she leaned back to a normally reserved composure then said to her, "You must learn when to speak and when not to speak. You have to learn how and when to speak to men. Most importantly, do not speak up to men as it is a sign of disrespect and the mafia takes honour and disrespect strongly in their code." "Your face is in a bad shape," Maria say. "Let me go get you some ice to dull the pain. Do you care for some pain killer as well?"

"Yes, please," Carmela said. She thought about how kind-hearted Maria was to her. Maria went to the door, brought out her key and unlocked it as she exits the room. Soon she would hear the metal lock turning again. She was locked in. it would seem she won't be going anywhere for a long time. Her father was being tied up in a room and locked away. His fate she has no idea about and now she was locked up in a bedroom with a key.

Her reality kicked in that she was a prisoner. Fighting or getting the mafia angry will not help her situation and she also needed to get her father out? If she was going to have any success at all, she needed to be of good behaviour and follow the rules. She remembers what Maria said to her. She whispered for a reason that phrase "women stick together." She must have said that for a reason. Maybe she was on her side. She could not tell yet but her face hurt a lot and she could use the ice and pain killer. The plan to escape was to obey and follow their rules. It felt like a shitty plan but that is all that she had got.

Maria returns to the room with water, pain killer and ice. Carmela took the painkiller first and Maria ensures that she drank the entire bottle of water. "You need this to rehydrate my child." Maria took the ice and started to apply it on her face. She continued to give her lessons and survival tips to get along with the mafia. "Never ask too many questions," she says. Carmela got that and she continued to grow under Maria's guide. She finally finished with her face and told her to get some rest. "We will continue in the morning," Maria says to her.

As she was about to leave, Carmela asked her if she would lock her in the room. Maria looked at her with a smile then said, "I wish I could but I have to lock you inside. This is the wish of Don Vito."

"I understand," Carmela says as she goes to sleep.

Maria became her guide. Although she was always locked up in the room she found some comfort with Maria. Maria's dressing style is colourful but she likes to wear vintage clothes because it made her skin glow. She took Carmela under her wings as she showed her how to dress like the wife of a mafia boss. She taught her how to conduct herself amongst the men. All this time she had no privilege to know about her father. Carmela already had the worst thought about her father. She believed he was already dead and she was trying to find a way to move on until she would make her great escape. Whenever she tried to ask about her father Maria would caution her to be careful. She listens to Maria. She's full of light and kind in heart. Carmela enjoyed being in the company of Maria. That was the best part of her day. Whenever she is locked in the room with no one to speak with or interact with she slowly falls into depression and thoughts of being a prisoner. Maria's presence made her forget about everything she had to deal with at Don Vito's house.

Maria always reminded Carmela that her situation was temporary. She told her that she has a special place with the Mafia. Salvatore is the hire and being considered to marry him puts her highly in rank and respect. She needs to learn their ways so she does not get on the bad side of Don Vito. Carmela's wardrobe changed to fancy clothes and designers. She was given the best and most expensive makeup accessories, pendants, necklaces and earrings. They needed her to look royal and magisterial.

Maria told her she will not be involved in any dirty or shady dealing with the mafia. Her role is to keep up appearance and look stunning as always. Maria assured her that as long as she was around no hurt will come upon her. Carmela felt reassured by her words. What a kind soul is Maria? She often thought how such a person got caught up with Don Vito and the mafia but she had no idea and felt it would be unpleasant to ask her about how she got involved with them. The mafia deals in drugs sold in the market and are the major distributors and they also sold to the socialites in the city. The activities of the mafia does not suit the personality of Maria. Perhaps there was more to her than she knew about. Carmela was happy to have Maria in her corner. She was her guiding light and mentor while she was living in the house as a prisoner.

While she was in isolation in the room and being mentored by Maria, the Mafia looked through Carmela's file. They studied and tracked her past life.

They knew all her routines and activities. She was someone they could use and they had Maria to take her into the transformation process. They wanted to know her beyond what they have seen. Soon they discovered she had a rich educational background and a degree in accounting. They learnt that she was seasoned and a professional in accounting. The mafia sort to use her abilities with their books. Carmela worked as an accountant. That was the life she had before she got mixed up with the mafia as a prisoner. The mafia already covered her track by acquiring the firm she worked at and gave her a leave of absence so that no one goes looking for her whereabouts and raise flags about her false imprisonment. They knew she would want to return to that life so they made her an offer to work with them on their books. Carmela saw this as an opportunity to gain their trust and prove her loyalty.

Carmela knew if she was brought on board to work their books she would soon learn about their business dealings especially the flow of money. She is good at what she does as she would give advice and covered their tracks where they were exposed and vulnerable. She was able to use her knowledge to increase their earning and cut down spending's that were not yielding any profit for their empire.

Carmela believes that if she could complete her task without resisting from the pressure of the mafia, she would gain their confidence and trust. She was ready to play the long game that would secure her chance to escape the nightmare of the mafia.

INDIVIDUAL DESIRES

The mafia got Carmela to work on their books which she did diligently. It was an opportunity she never saw coming and when it came, she knew it was her best option if she had any thought to escape. She worked on their books not because she wanted to help the mafia but because she needed to gain their trust so that she could plan a proper escape from the mafia world. Her impact was immediately noticed as their profits went higher. She saw through their shady dealings and their money flows. She knew the names of those on their payroll and how much they earned. The mafia was earning in millions daily from illegal activities and business they had taken over. She saw through all their money laundry activities but she had no choice to continue with such job for the mafia as it came with the territory. Carmela thought it would be for a short while but rather it started from days then it extended into months. Carmela thought working for the mafia would mean she will get some freedom to go outside as she was confined to the room. She was surprised that they made a workspace for her in the room. She had to do everything manually without using any computer or any sort of internet connection. She worked on papers with a pen and a calculator. Her workspace had a large table and enough lighting to enable her to work at any point in time. All through the time she worked on their books, Carmela was locked up all the time. Carmela began to think if Maria was also locked up before accepting her fate. She kept on working and balancing their books. Checking for discrepancies in their books and identifying them. Those stealing from the mafia got exposed but she had no idea that she did that. All she knew was she saw things that did not add up and reported it to her supervisor who would be her future husband. Carmela had no idea that the mafia executed those that stole from them. She was slowly gaining their trust without knowing it. The member of the mafia did not know who was behind the account but they already gave her a nickname called The Accountant. Once they heard the books were going to The Accountant, those that stole either made a run for it or prayed that they didn't get caught. Things began to change in the mafia and the stealing from Don Vito stopped. Carmela was able to hide their money flow and also erase their money trails that could expose the organisation. Because she worked in isolation most of the time she could not tell if it was day or night. She could not tell if the sun was up or the moon was bright in the sky. They would not let her see any of these and it sometimes drove her crazy. Maria always made her feel good when she was around. It was the only time she felt like she was not losing her mind.

She works with no pressure although Salvatore always watched her every step. Carmela knows that he doesn't know what she is up to but the mafia wanted her to always be supervised at all time. Salvatore was never chatty with her while they were always together for most of the time. He sits on the leather chair and observes her while making calls and keeping up with the business. From time to time he would get coffee from the help. Breakfast, brunch or dinner. Carmela could never tell but she could suspect the time of the day depending on the food brought to Salvatore. Days where he took English breakfast could mean it was in the morning. He is her supposed future husband that she expected would want to get to know her. It's been days and months but they barely exchange words or had any conversations. Although whenever he is around, he doesn't lock the door to the room. This gesture alone does not make her feel like a prisoner even though she always felt like one. Sometimes he would step out of the room for a private phone call and still leave the door unlocked. Maybe he trusts her. Maybe he was testing her. She could never tell as for all the times he never engaged her in a proper conversation. Somehow, she felt comfortable under his watchful eye. Unlike Don Vito that scares her with his appearance alone. She could not imagine working and being watched by him. Salvatore is tall at a 5'10 and has an arrogant air about him which she could not decipher but he is a tanned skin man. He looked like his father with his thin eyebrows, flat nose and small lips but unlike his father, he had a long face with a cleft chin.

But tonight Salvatore didn't pay more attention to her. He was distracted as he puffed his cigar and looked into the distance in deep thoughts. It would seem he was lost but his presence was still in the room as he sat on the leather chair at the corner of the room where he normally sits to watch over Carmela as she worked on the books. Carmela had questions but Maria had warned her not to ask any question that would get her into any trouble. Carmela had been in good nature with the mafia and everyone without causing any trouble. She wanted to keep that going but she was worried about stepping out of line. But she could not help to be concerned about Salvatore that was lost in thought and his face was different from the other times he had been around. Salvatore continued to puff his cigarette which was helped tightly in between his two fingers.

"Are you alright?" her soft sweet voice travelled to the edge of the room where he was and it got his attention as he snaps back to reality from his distant gaze. It was as though his mind was somewhere else and her voice returned him to his body.

Salvatore's gaze shifted towards her. His eyes looked into hers and it was the first time he would look directly at her that way. Carmela caught a grip of fear in her heart. She began to get worried that she had crossed a line. She hasn't been struck by fear in a long time since her encounter with Don Vito in that room. She began to think of the worst scenario like her experience with Don Vito that slapped her. Maybe she would end the night with a black eye ws what she thought.

But all of her fears went away when he smiled back at her brightly. She had never seen him smile and it was delightful and warming. Her worries flew out of the window at the instant.

He leaned forward and stood up from the leather chair tucked in the corner. He took his steps slowly as he made his way over to her in the room. Carmela sat and watched him come her way. His frame was much more seen and appreciate by her and she could see his long arms and short wavy hair. His clothing was no different from other days. He wore his regular black and well fitted high-end clothes that were perfectly pressed.

Then he asked an unexpected question. It caught Carmela by surprise.

He says to her, "Tell me. . ."

"What are your greatest desires?" There was a short silence in the room then he goes further to break the silence by assuring her that whatever her answer would be a secret between the two of them and it will never leave the room.

Carmela was unsure of what to say but she knew she had to say something. "My answer will be a secret right?" she responded for more assurance as her fingers were dancing on the calculator. Salvatore assured her again and she felt it was a safe space to say what she wanted.

Salvatore was known to have an egotistical flaw but he somehow was cool with her tonight. The tone in the room was comforting and Carmela knew it was a good opportunity to state her desires.

Carmela's fingers stop dancing across the keys of the calculator, as she puts down her pen.

She looked at him intently to tell him her greatest desires and what she wanted.

"So," Carmela spoke with a little shyness. "My greatest desire is to go home. And more, I want to return home with my father. It's not my place to ask but I hope he is still alive so we could return together."

He walks over to her side not saying any word yet but he had a smile on his face and his hand still had his cigarette in his finger. He walked over to the side of her desk and moves some books and papers to the side to allow himself to sit on the desk then he crossed his legs. Carmela slowly without being noticed, pushed herself backwards with the chair she sat on such that Salvatore would not hear her deep breath that was obvious as she exhaled deeply. She did it respectably not to trigger Salvatore in any way. Her eyes showed a lot of fear and Salvatore saw through her.

He saw her fears as she was shaken up by what she said. So he reassured her not to be afraid. She had nothing to worry about. This is a safe place and our conversation is just between the two of us and no one else. I assure you that this will never leave the room. Carmela's breathing began to normalise and her heartbeat came to its normal tempo. It was as though a heavy burden was lifted from her chest.

So he reassured her not to be afraid. She had nothing to worry about. "This is a safe place and our conversation is just between the two of us and no one else. I assure you that this will never leave the room."

Carmela's breathing began to normalise and her heartbeat came to its normal tempo. It was as though a heavy burden was lifted from her chest.

Then there was a moment of silence in the room. The only sound was the ticking swatch watch on Salvatore's hand followed by their breath which could be heard as the room was silent while they both gazed into each other's eyes for the second time tonight.

Then he asked her, "Tell me Carmela . . ." he says. "Tell me about your former life. What was life for you on the other side?" he asked her genuinely wanting to know. Carmela could see that he was truly interested in her story. Then he asked further and more specifically, "Carmela," he calls her name softly as he spoke. "Have you ever been in love? Have you loved someone or are you in a relationship with somebody." She had never been asked any personal question since she was held captive at Don Vito's house.

Their eyes were still fixed on each other then she says, "I can't recall ever being in love but I have had a few relationships. There was no serious relationship going but I can only admit that they were all short term relationships. I have never had that feeling of love and I have never had to express deeply with anyone."

"What about your mother?"

Carmela's eyes went off and her countenance changed. Salvatore could tell that she was disgusted at the thought of her mother.

Salvatore read the room but before he could say anything Carmela answer with disgust. "She is dead to me. I don't want to talk about her. Can we talk about something else?" she asks him as her mood was getting disturbed. Salvatore understood that her mother must have been a deadbeat.

Salvatore leans back as he puffed his cigarette to let out a smoke ring. Then he says to her, "I have once been in love. I was young and naive. It went well for a while but she broke it off. She broke my heart. For that reason, I had no choice but to kill her."

Carmela was shocked and motivated by fear.

Then she asked him, "Will this be my ultimate fate?" Salvatore puffed his cigarette and lets out another smoke ring.

Then he said to her, "Time will tell." He repeated it as though his voice should echo, "Time will tell..."

We would have to wait and see. His response seemed cold and different from the man that seemed concerned earlier and wanted to know about her past life.

Salvatore looks at his wrist to check the time. "You have to finish up now. I have other pending matter that needs my attention." He started to walk back to his seat and continued to smoke. Carmela was a little scared about what he said but she continued with her work. Moments later, she finished up wrong on the books and informed him about it. Salvatore checks her out for work completed then he leaves but not without locking her in the room. Carmela was once again by herself as she thought about her plans to gain the trust of the mafia but it would seem Salvatore maybe an issue. He knows her deepest desires. He knows she wants to leave the mafia. Her questions and desires could seem she is not interested in getting married to him. But Maria had warned her of not asking questions and making request. She began to think of what ifs. *"What if she had given away her wild car?*

What if Salvatore goes against his words and tells his father of her desires. What if?"

She went over to the king sized bed with a clear thought. If he was going to sell her out, he would have done that already. She didn't worry much as she was set to relax from her day's work. She had earned the trust of the mafia and soon she would be let out to move freely. Her plans were steadily set into motion and she will not let anything distract her from her goals. She had to stay focus and do what was asked of her by the mafia or anyone. Maria has taught her well, it is up to her to continue in her good behaviour.

TEMPTATION

Slowly as she had planned Carmela had no guards on her watch. She was no longer isolated and locked in the room. She could go in and out but not to exceed the limit of the property. She could walk around unsupervised yet she was never alone whenever she had to take a walk. Cameras were watching but she knew better not to make a run for it yet as she was still gathering more information and gaining more of the trust of the mafia. At the centre of the compound is a magnificent statue of a black lion. The lion is surrounded with water and it had its lighting that is colourful at night and the most important and unique feature about it is the fountain. It is just at the middle facing the main entrance and just at the tip of the curve of the driveway that leads up to the main house.

She was becoming an asset to the mafia. The face of "The Account" was now known. She grew a reputation for herself as the eyes of the mafia in their finances. The mafia grew larger with their assets because of her accounting talents on their funds and investments. She got everything right and spot-on that mafia recorded no financial loss in that quarter. Maria often would walk with her and reminds her that women stick together. Maria was her companion at the house. Carmela was still set to marry Salvatore but she was still in the loop of what was going on and when it would happen. Perhaps she was still being watched. Carmela had done everything as she was sure she had their trust. But she would have to be more consistent to gain their trustfully. The mafia is unforgiving to anyone who goes against them. She knew if she had to escape she must not have a reason to turn back.

She would walk around the house, the gardens and often time enjoy the opulent view of the scenery.

She knew her place and what was expected of her. She spoke less and reacted less to anything that bothered her which could come off as disrespect to the men, the mafia, Salvatore and Don Vito. It was hard at a glance but it got easier over time. Carmela detested the mafia and it was hard keeping up appearances like she was one of them and living their home. She saw the woman she was slowly fading away. The woman she used to be was almost gone. She needed saving. She needed to be out of there before she loses who she is to the woman she was becoming, but there was nothing she could do but to be patient and trust the process of her plan.

Salvatore was always with her whenever Maria was not with Carmela. Carmela knew she could talk to Salvatore just about anything but she would not push her luck. He kept to his word and never spoke about their discussion to anyone from that night. Soon she began to spend more time with Salvatore.

She had proven her loyalty to Don Vito. The Don approved of her but never showed it. Carmela never knew about this so she kept working harder and behaving herself to be approved.

As she grew closer with Salvatore, they took more walks and ate dinners together. Maria saw them both and she appreciated it. She like seeing her son with Carmela. At night, Maria would gossip with her son about Carmela while teasing him about seeing them together. She'll pry to try to get some words out of him but Salvatore doesn't say much to her but laugh it off. She would tease some more about their growing relationship and closeness.

Carmela continued to work on the books for the mafia and keeping it balanced. She needed to keep the money trail invisible. The mafia had created an office for her that she no longer had to work from her room and locked up inside. The difference with her false imprisonment was an upgrade to her privileges. She didn't let it get the best of her that she had freedom. She was still a prisoner of the mafia. On her way to the office on a certain cold night, Carmela began to hear loud noises down the hall. She stops and listens closely. The noise got louder. What could be happening she thought? Should I find out? She began to walk slowly without making any noise. With every step that she took, the foul languages got louder. And as she got closer the noise got familiar as she could make out the voices of the parties involved. She could recognize their voices. It was Don Vito and Salvatore.

What could be the cause of this heated argument between father and son? Carmela wanted to eavesdrop but she knew the price if she was caught. She began to backtrack in a haste without making any sound to return to the office.

She sat at her workplace wishing she had eavesdropped on their argument. But she was left only with her thoughts she could never know what it was all about.

She began to play with the keys of the calculator. She was getting focused with a job trying to mind her business when suddenly the door to the office opens wide and she saw his frame occupying the opened space. Salvatore enters the room and closes the door behind him.

He looks at her then says, "You heard our conversations." Carmela turns to him and swears she did not listen to them. Salvatore looks at her then says, "I believe you." She could tell he was very furious and upset at the same time. He unbuttons the collar of his shirt as though it prevented him from breathing fine. Then he takes the armrest of the leather chair furiously and unconsciously. Carmela notices his gesture but she knew trying to calm him down could worsen the situation and so she was quiet and observing. He continues this way them he looked at her again.

Carmela could tell he was about to ask her a question.

Salvatore asks her, first by calling her, "Carmela!"

"Yes," she responds

"How far are you willing to go for your freedom? What can you do to earn your freedom?"

This seemed like the opportunity she always wanted. This looked too easy and too good to be true. But she replies, "It depends on what I'll have to do." Salvatore and Carmela had become close that she was confident in their relationship.

Then he dropped a bomb on her; he asked her if she was ready to kill for her freedom. Carmela was dumbfounded and shocked at the same time. Her mouth was opened wide for a minute.

She held onto her thought and hoped he was pulling and expensive joke but it would seem he was serious. She did not know what to say or do as she was left in a state of her own unable to speak. Salvatore stood up from his chair and strode from his usual corner in the room to towards Carmela.

The office looked similar to Carmela's room but the only difference was the absence of a bed. However, the office had its unique features. It had sturdy bookshelves that lined the walls as the expensive wood desk is placed in the middle of them, closer to the window. Carmela's office had window which she could use to view the outside world. It had a beautiful rug that covers the hardwood floors and protects the floor from the heavy filing cabinet. There is a cash machine on a long wood table which she makes use of when she started handling cash and going to the bank. She had a paper shredder which she requested for to work it. The office was style in the 80's settings. It smelled of paper and oil perfume. He walked towards her desk with his eyes fixed on her. Then he gives her a sweet and confident smile as though she had accepted to do what he wanted. Perhaps, he believed she would do anything and he felt more confident about this.

More deliberately this time, he asks, "Would you kill for me? Would you kill for me to earn your freedom?" Carmela couldn't help but wonder why Salvatore could not kill the person through the use of hired guns. Why would he want a fragile woman to carry out this job? She had no answers as she could not think of any.

"If you do this for me, I will ensure your freedom and safety. You won't have to look over your shoulder anymore or worry that the mafia would want their pound of flesh. I will ensure you have no ties with the mafia. You will have your full freedom."

This seemed impossible and suddenly she began to see through his objective. The only way this could be done is if Don Vito was no longer in the picture. She thought deeply until she was interrupted by Salvatore.

Then he said to her, "If you can kill my family, I will make your desires come true. I'll have all the power to make it happen and level you up if you choose to do this for me." This was their safe place and she knew whatever they talked about was confidential.

Carmela never saw herself as a killer but desperate time's calls for desperate measures. Her hand was squeezing unto a paper that made ruffled sounds. Soon she realises what she was doing and stops. Her thought was she could be doing something she never thought she would ever do. Taking a life would be very difficult but freedom was the price to be earned. All she had to do was kill his family, but who exactly? She had no idea, Salvatore did not give her enough information going forward. She was yet to verbally agree to this but from her body language Salvatore could tell that she was down for this. She could sense the desperation in her ever since she told him of her deepest desires for freedom. He needed to use her desperation for both of them to benefit from this endeavour. Salvatore walked away while leaving her at the bridge of choices and decisions. The following day while she was taken a walk in the house, Carmela would run into a face. A member of the Agresti family. She ran into Matteo who does not approve of her. He considers her weak and not worthy to be part of their family. Everyone knew he disliked Carmela but she could not understand why he did. Matteo always suspected Carmela? He believed she was up to something and Carmela often feared that he could ruin her plan to escape. Everyone in the mafia had no issues with him except for Matteo. He often insisted openly that she cannot be trusted especially with their books. He saw through Carmela that she could be a threat. He had no idea of her end game but he always had one eye on her. Carmela felt uncomfortable at the house whenever he was around. She had to deal with and keep up appearance every day while watching over her shoulder from slipping because of Salvatore's younger brother.

Mateo Agresti is more feared than his brother. He was ruthless in the field and he got things done for the mafia through intimidation, killing, blackmailing and bribes. He had several high stakes official in his pocket that gave the mafia an edge. Often times the men in the mafia preferred Matteo's leadership to Salvatore. They believed Matteo was the true hire to the empire although he was year younger. There were other factions that wanted Salvatore. These brothers act like mortal enemies which made them grow stringer independently trying to outdo each other in everything and in every other manner.

Matteo keeping tabs on Carmela was trouble and now that he had returned from his long trip for the mafia, he was going to be around for a very long time.

He said to Carmela when he ran into her in the hallway, "I have got my eyes on you. I will find out what you are up to soon enough and my father will know I was right about you all along. You may have fooled my mother, my stupid and naïve brother including my father and everyone else around but you haven't fooled me. I see through you and I am never wrong. Watch out for me. I am coming to you."

As he was about to tell the situation of her father and what happened to him, a voice came from behind of Carmela. It was Salvatore. He said to her, "I hope he is not bothering you in any way."

Before she replied Matteo jumped in and said, "I was just congratulating your wife to be," with a fake smile and grin. "Welcome to the Agresti family. I should be on my way brother. See you around, Carmela." Then he left.

Carmela was speechless but Salvatore was there to comfort her and told her not to be worried or get bothered by whatever his brother says. "He is a pain and he causes trouble everywhere. Come with me," he says to Carmela and they both continued together to have dinner that night.

DARK MOMENTS

Salvatore and Carmela's relationship continued to grow like a tree. They were solid and deep for one another like taproots. Carmela never thought she would be fond of him. But here she was with the son of the man that made her a prisoner. She was fond of the first son of the Agresti family. The same family that is responsible for the fate of her father. She had been at the house for months yet no one ever mentioned or said anything about her father and she dared not ask about him. Salvatore often gave her gifts. He gave her different kinds such as clothes, flowers and more.

Salvatore's brother who was mostly in the field did not like seeing them together. Matteo and Salvatore did not get along very well. Since they were kids, they had always been rivals. Their sibling rivalry grew till they were old. Although the difference between them in age is one year gap, oftentimes they were mostly seen as twins to outsiders. Salvatore hated this while growing up. Matteo was more involved in the mafia work and he was also a hitman for the mafia. He had a height advantage when fighting because he is 6 ft tall. Like his mother, he had olive skin and his countenance was as though that of a man that was frustrated. They both had a grudge that no one could identify the real cause of it. They were both set on a path that could bring an end to either one of them when given the chance.

Matteo never liked Carmela. He doesn't think she is worthy to be part of the mafia. He believes she is weak and he made this known to Salvatore who got angry at him for saying such words about her. Salvatore knows his brother very well and he knows how to get him without being noticed.

Salvatore and Carmela's relationship continued to grow. Carmela never thought she would be fond of him. But here she was with the son of the man that made her a prisoner. Salvatore often gave her gifts. He gave her different kinds such as clothes, flowers and more.

He had a simple and well thought out plan and he was going to use Carmela to make this happen. No one would suspect foul play. He bought Carmela a gift which was wrapped in a huge red box with white ribbons. She opens it up revealing a beautiful pair of gloves. "Wow! These are lovely. Thank you, Salvatore," and she openly embraces him.

"I want you to wear these gloves every time you go out. There are enough gloves in the box that you could change into match your clothing."

"Thank you once again," Carmela thanked him gladly.

Don Vito heard about the gift of the beautiful gloves Salvatore gave his soon to be blushing bride and thought they were merely a gift from the heart. But he never questioned the intention.

Carmela was eluded of the intentions Salvatore had about the gloves. Salvatore's plans were already in motion. Matteo was keeping tabs on Carmela which gave Salvatore the chance to move discretely with his plans. He knew where Matteo kept his weapons. He knew their location and how to access them. Salvatore stole his brothers favourite gun and held unto it until he had alone time with Carmela at night.

Carmela expected him that night as she always does. He came in and sat on his favourite chair in the room while he fluffed some smoke and let out some smoke ring in the process. She had a feeling about Salvatore tonight but what was it? Salvatore went straight to her and present the weapon.

"A gun!" Carmela exclaimed but silently.

"Do you want your freedom or not?" Salvatore responded. "There is a price for everything and this is your key to it. But first, you need to wear your gloves before you ever touch this weapon."

Carmela now got a clear perspective to why he got her the gift. She collected the gun and hid it somewhere safe.

No one was searching for her or monitoring her except for Matteo who got his eyes on her. Carmela had been going to the banks by herself and running personal errands. She had gained the trust of the mafia but she needed a clean escape from them. She could go out by herself anywhere she wanted. It would seem she had freedom but what she had was an illusion of freedom.

Salvatore says to her again, "Remember to wear your glove at all times when you are handling this weapon." She nods her head in acknowledgement. She knew not who owned the weapon and she never bothered to ask about it.

Then she asked him, "What am I to do with this weapon? Protect myself or ..."

"Or you are going to use this to earn your freedom Salvatore," he completed her sentence. "You are going to kill Maria."

"What! No! It can't be her. Why her?"

"That's not important," Salvatore says. "The important thing is that you will do it." He broke down the plans for her and how to go about it. Carmela could not believe what she was about to do. "What you have to do is follow Maria and shoot her. Get away from the scene and return the weapon to me. Can you do that?" Carmela nodded again in agreement. "You can do this," he continued to encourage her. "Do not think about it too much? Don't panic, okay. You can handle a gun, right?"

"Yes, I can," Carmela responded.

Her father used to take her to the shooting range when she was younger. She knew how to handle a gun and she has a very good aim when it comes to shooting. The mafia and no one else knew about this and so she would never be a suspect to any murder involving a shooting if an investigation were to be carried out. Carmela needed some time to process this. This would be her first killing. She had never killed anyone and moreso she was asked to kill Maria.

Carmela could only think of why Salvatore wanted Maria dead. She thought he wanted Don Vito dead, but Maria? It broke her heart. She knew what she had to do, when and where it would take place. Maria was the only person that first cared for her and was her only friend. She was there when she was down. She had a gun in her hand and was set to kill her.

The day came after a week of planning and the schedule was in order. Maria went to the salon while Carmela went to the bank. They both left separately at different time intervals. Carmela had to be quick with are back runs so that she could drive over to where Maria was doing her hair.

She had the gun and was hyperventilating. She later controlled her breathing by taking in deep breaths to stabilise.

Carmela began to cry in her heart. Maria was everything to her. She helped her in transitioning into this new life and she showed her unmatched kindness.

Carmela and Salvatore were also scheduled for lunch at a restaurant in the city close by. Salvatore was already at the restaurant waiting for Carmela. Carmela was outside of the Salon anticipating Maria to come out. A few moments later, Maria comes out looking happy. The timing was perfect as it was not so long she had left the bank and some few minutes that Maria was done at the salon.

The timing couldn't be more perfect. Carmela looks over the frame of her designer sunglasses and watches Maria walk towards her car, currently parked in a parking lot, towards Carmela. Carmela's breathing staggers as her heart races, her hands sweaty in the gloves. She can hear Maria's heels click, the sound getting louder as she approaches the car. When Carmela feels she's close enough, she climbs out of the car; the gun tucked away in her trench coat pocket. Maria sees her future daughter-in-law and smiles, ready to say hello. Her face was as bright as the sun with her cheerful heart being excited to see Carmela.

But before Maria could get any closer, as though it was second nature. Carmela pulls the gun out and presses on the trigger with a drop of tears rolling down her cheek with what she had done. The gun kicks back and Carmela watches Maria fall to the ground as the bullet hit her. Her sunglasses had fallen off her head. The sound of the gunshot echoed. Carmela rushes back to her car and does her best to calmly drive away as though nothing had just happened. She used her rare mirror and saw Maria's lifeless body. There was no going back. She had done the unthinkable. She focused on the road as she went to meet up with Salvatore.

The body was left out in the open to be easily discovered. Carmela arrived at the restaurant to meet up with Salvatore discretely without drawing any suspicion. "Is it done?" he asked her. She nodded to affirm that it was done. Carmela was shaken-up by this but Salvatore was with her to calm her nerves. She slipped the weapon to him in a cloth wrapped like a gift. They both had lunch together as though nothing had happened before returning to the house. When they arrived there was no news or report about Maria. Salvatore went ahead to return the weapon where he found it. It was nightfall and Maria had not returned to the house. This got everyone but Carmela and Salvatore worried as they both knew what had happened. Don Vito thought a rival gang had gotten to her and perhaps they will demand a ransom. A team of search party was put together to find his wife but they all returned with no positive information.

Later the next day, the news of her death was everywhere and Don Vito was very angry. He vowed to kill anyone who was responsible for her death even if it was family. He never goes against his word. He adored Maria more than anyone else. He was thirsty for blood and revenge. That next evening, after the news struck the core of the mafia and Don Vito's heart, mistrust and allegations spread through the ranks like wildfire. But thanks to inside contacts within the local police, Don Vito was able to get some information on the killing. Carmela sat in her room, unable to sleep. She was scared that it could come back to bite her.

"What have I done?" she said speaking to herself.

Suddenly, she hears a knock on her door that scared her. Salvatore let himself into the room and walks into her bedroom with blood on his shirt. Carmela jumps from the bed and rushes over to him, immediately looking to see if he's hurt. But rather he grabbed her and kissed her instead. Carmela did not understand what was going on. "What happened?" she asked him.

"Matteo is dead!" Carmela was shocked at the news.

"How did they get to him?" she asked.

"No one got to him. My father killed him. The murder weapon belongs to Matteo. I stole it to set him up. The bullet found was registered to the murder weapon belonging to my brother. My father found out as I expected he would and so he killed him." Salvatore smiled as he told her. Carmela did not know how to feel. She was indifferent.

"I keep to my words. I am a man of my words," Salvatore said to her. "From tomorrow, you will be free."

Carmela could not understand how this could be possible. She had questions but Salvatore told her to save it for later. He let himself out of the room and closed the door behind him. Everything was happening too fast. Freedom was just a day away and she looked forward to seeing the light of a new day.

ACT 3

PERSONAL SACRIFICE

With two members of the Agresti family dead, it was truly a dark time in the household. The mafia were shaken up by the tragic event as if things couldn't get any uglier. They had no one to suspect especially since the death of Matteo. Don Vito killing his son sent a deep message to the entire mafia that no one is above his punishment. Fear loomed over the mafia along with darkness and mourning. Everyone loved Maria, she was a gentle and sweet soul that looked out on the best of others.

Killing Maria broke something in Carmela. She felt damage as though she lost a part of her humanity. But she had agreed to help Salvatore kill his family. Salvatore was the only one who knew about Carmela's skills with the gun. She looked frail as though she was not capable of hurting a fly. It was the impression that people often had when they meet with her. She knew people saw her as weak but her father brought her up to be a strong and independent woman.

Being isolated and the false prison created a strong resolve in her that she longed seek for revenge. When the opportunity showed up her subconscious kicked into auto drive and she began to take in every opportunity she had to get back at the mafia. Maria was a huge collateral damage for her goal. Killing Maria created a ripple effect that opened up an opportunity to get closer to Don Vito who was not in a pleasant mood and wanted to be left alone. The mafia took everything from her and she was determined to get back at them somehow for everything they took from her. Her father was her only family yet they could not give her the privilege to bid him a proper welfare even at death. They never gave her the information she needed. When she asked about her father, she was told it was disrespectful. That statement was distasteful to her and she hated it. She hated being told what to do and what to say. It took so long but she was happy to see how it played out.

She always had these words in her heart, *patience is a virtue*.

Carmela had played the long game and it had favoured her. Her freedom was set for the morning and she would have all the time in the world for herself. She had dreamt of riding into the sunset of freedom on the back of a stallion. Riding away to her destiny, to her goal. To riding away from the life of criminal activity. It was like a dream, a blur that seemed unreal but she had come too far. She could smell her freedom. Carmela knew her father was already dead as the mafia hid the truth from her all this time. She knew he was killed the last time she saw him. The last memory of her father was unpleasant and she hated that memory of him. She remembers the picture of him bleeding to death by Don Vito's orders. What hurt her the most was she never got to know the reason why he was killed. She was also forced into this life as they took away her rights and freedom. She avoided the truth but the truth was right in front of her. She wanted revenge and she got the revenge somehow when members of the Agresti family got killed. She was involved in their death directly or indirectly as in the case of Matteo who died because she killed Maria with his favourite hand gun. It happened in a way she wasn't anticipating. All she wanted to do from the beginning was to run away with a father and never look back but she's now caught up with the world of the mafia. She had one final thing in mind to do.

She needed to be fully free. Freedom comes at a price, she had to learn the hard way. She has paid for her freedom but what is freedom if you are running away from something. Her life had changed over the months. She had lived a different life and it started to become a part of her. She was becoming what she never wanted to be. This happened day by day as she was mentally conditioned by the mafia.

Don Vito was sad and in a depressed mood after losing his wife. The Don had never been in such a state. But he was cold and angry but mostly depressed. Carmela goes up to the kitchen to collect the food tray that was meant to be taken up to him. She tells the maid not to worry about carrying it up that she has it all covered. The maid was happy to let her carry the tray up. None of the maids wanted to take up the food tray to Don Vito's office as they were scared of him. Most of the time the maids tried to avoid the duty of taken his food up to him. Whenever Maria was around, they would be happy because she would take it up to him. Don Vito could slap a maid for the slightest reason that got him irritated and none of them could tell what could upset him. Sometimes the reason could be ridiculous such as if he doesn't like the face of the maid. He could hit or have her fired immediately. Carmela volunteering with her high position in the mafia was such a huge relief. They were happy she wanted to deliver the food to him in person.

She carried the tray up the flight of stairs to Don Vito's office. His office had large doors and security cameras. She puts the tray on one hand as she proceeds to knock on the door.

Carmela stands before Don Vito's closed office doors. She closed her eyes for a brief moment to knock on the door. She took a deep breath and felt confident.

She knocks on the door twice with little effort but there was no response. Maybe she wasn't making enough sound so she tried again. She knocks again but much louder and she would hear a voice coming from the office instructing her to come inside. She came into his intimidating presence but not this time. She was no longer intimidated by him. She was on a mission. No distraction, just pure focus.

He hasn't spoken to anyone all day since he got the news about Maria's death. There was silence in the room before she entered the room, she could tell.

When she came inside the office after being told by him to enter, Don Vito yelled at her that he doesn't want to be bothered with a squeaky voice.

"But I brought you something to eat. You haven't eaten any food all day and you could use something to replenish your energy." So he allows her to come into the office completely as she was standing by the door with a hand gesture. He did not look her way as she came into the room with the food in her hand.

Carmela walked in with the food in her hand but she struggled to balance the food in the tray. She had to cover the slight bump under her shirt. She hopes Don Vito won't notice. But he wasn't looking at her or paying attention to what she was doing. She noticed he wasn't looking so she did not worry if he would notice anything as he was engrossed with what he was doing. It would seem he was engrossed with what he was holding; she couldn't make out what it was from where she was. But as she approached his desk with each step, she could feel the cold barrel of the gun press gently against her tailbone. She was unnerved, she was confident and ready for what would happen next. She had already played it over in her head. It was all left to her to execute it.

She was getting close to him to have a closer range. She was sure of her aim but she needed the shot to be closer so could achieve what she wanted.

Don Vito doesn't look at her, keeping his eyes down, looking at his wedding picture with Maria. He drifted into a daydream and thoughts of his time with his wife. He remembered all the time they had together. She was always there to calm his nerves whenever he lost his temper. Her death broke him internally but he is a man that shows no weakness. His hand was all over the photo when Carmela dropped the food tray in front of him that caught his attention. But he didn't look up to her yet, he thanked her and continued gazing at the photo. Carmela has had enough of him and his depressed state that it did not mean anything to her as she pulled out the gun and points it on his head. Don Vito felt the cold barrel of her gun. Before he could make any move or say a word Carmela blasted his brains out and his head fell into the food. His brain membrane scattered and there was blood spill everywhere. She had put the gun on the side of his head before shooting it.

Immediately she removes the glove on her hand them puts the gun in Don Vito's hand. She hides the gloves properly so no one would suspect a thing.

Carmela began to scream at the sight of his lifeless body. Don Vito's room has no camera which she had envisaged before doing this final mission as payback for her father. Her scream was loud that Salvatore came running along with other members of the mafia. They rushed into the room to find their boss dead. He had committed suicide as it would seem. They saw the blood all over the place and the terrified Carmela

She became hysterical as she was explaining that she brought him some food to eat because he hadn't eaten all day and has been rejecting every food that was brought to him by the maids. She began to shake as though she was experiencing a shock and it seemed so real.

"He was right there saying nothing as he was looking into that picture," she pointed at the wedding picture. Carmela continued to describe what she had seen as tears flowed down her eyes. The mafia security detail was holding their weapons but Salvatore instructed them to lower their weapons.

He told them to clean up the place and cover the death of his father. He doesn't want the news of his father dying by suicide to be out there. The clean-up crew knew how to handle situations such as this. Salvatore took her in his arms and escorts her out of the room while lacing his fingers into her hair. They continued to walk together to Carmela's room. They got to the room and Carmela pulls him closer to embrace him.

Salvatore told her he is ready to live up to the end of their deal. He got more than he wanted. The death of his family and he would gain the entire control of the empire. You can leave tomorrow morning. He leads her to her room as a gentleman. He opens her bedroom door and to his surprise, playfully, Carmela pulls Salvatore into her room, he wraps his arms around her waist. They were close up with no space between them. Just their gaze fixed on each other as they had been doing for months. Carmela thanks him for the offer, but she'd like to stay. She couldn't think of living in a world without him. She wanted of him.

"They is no point hiding our feelings anymore," she says. His eyes said so many things as she looked deep into his eyes. More importantly, she wants to get married to him. She told him how she felt. This was her life now and she knew no way to return to her past life. She is a new person with new wants and desires. Salvatore was happy that she wanted to stay.

"This is what I wanted. I have fallen into you," Salvatore expressed himself.

"So have I, I feel the same way too," Carmela acknowledged this to him. Salvatore leans in for a soft kiss but Carmela grabbed him and kissed him passionately into the night. He held her and kissed her back. They both laughed as they continued to kiss.

"It has been so long coming," Salvatore said. "I'm happy to be here with you. To share this feeling," he smiled and planted a wet kiss on her forehead.

But Carmela wasn't going to be satisfied until she gets what she wanted. "I want us to get married right away," Carmela demanded from Salvatore. Salvatore expressed his concerns that he just lost member of his family but Carmela insisted. She immediately called the priest at the local church and started to make preparations for the wedding. Salvatore could not fight her because he liked Carmela. She told him that the only way the mafia would respect her is she was legally married. And so that evening the priest arrived and with the presence of some witnesses in the mafia at the gazebo at the Agresti house.

The wedding ceremony began and it was small wedding as Carmela forced his hands. It was decorated on a short notice with white flowers, just as Carmela wanted. Her stylist came through for her with an elegant wedding dress and Salvatore was radiant in his black tuxedo. And in the presence of the mafia and their affiliate that were invited to the wedding. The priest blessed them as they read their wedding vows then he pronounced them husband and wife. The audience clapped for them and congratulated them as the newest couples. The witnesses murmurs that it was a good idea to restructure the Agresti house as it was shaken by a dark storm.

Salvatore resumed control of the mafia empire with Carmela by his side. Together they started a new generation of the Agresti family and built a mighty dynasty.